Pirates of the Purple Dawn

by Tony Abbott

Illustrated by Royce Fitzgerald

Cover illustration by Tim Jessell

A
LITTLE APPLE
PAPERBACK

SCHOLASTIC INC.
New York Toronto London Auckland Sydney
Mexico City New Delhi Hong Kong Buenos Aires

For My Family

For more information about the continuing saga of Droon,
please visit Tony Abbott's website at
www.tonyabbottbooks.com

ISBN-13: 978-0-439-90250-2
ISBN-10: 0-439-90250-9

12 11 10 9 8 7 6 5 4 3 2 1   7 8 9 10 11 12/0

Printed in the U.S.A.
First printing, February 2007

Contents

One

The Vision Thing

When Eric Hinkle found himself in a creepy tunnel, with weird, hissing noises all around him, he realized he would much rather be in school.

"Oh, yeah," he said to himself. "I'd be at my desk, Neal and Julie would be just two seats away, with Mrs. Michaels up there, teaching stuff, maybe even giving us a quiz. Really, I'd be fine with a quiz! But no . . ."

No. Eric wasn't in school.

In fact, he was as far away from class as it was possible to be. Jagged, rocky walls pressed on him from every side. He could barely see a thing. His feet hurt. His head throbbed. He felt sick.

"Yeah, and what's *that*?" he wondered.

He could just make out an odd green haze drifting in the darkness ahead. And now and again he could smell something.

What was it? Apples?

"Apples! Like at my house!" he said, recalling the trees outside his bedroom window.

But Eric wasn't near his house, either. He was somewhere else entirely. He was in the fantastic, magical, and secret world of Droon.

Of course, he was in Droon. Where else would a weird old tunnel be?

"But if I'm in Droon," he asked, "where

are Julie and Neal? They're always with me."

Just then, as if in answer to his question, he heard a whisper in his ear and felt a tap on his shoulder. But when he turned around, no one was there. "Okay, I really don't like this place!" Eric said out loud.

When he turned around to face forward again, Eric was startled to see the shape of a tall figure moving toward him. The green haze poured from it like smoke from a fire. And the smell of apples was stronger than ever.

"Wh-wh-who are you?" he stammered.

In a low voice that sounded as if it could belong to either a man or a woman — *or neither* — the figure spoke. "Look here!"

A thin hand rose up from the silhouette and pointed behind it. Squinting into the shadows, Eric saw . . . a map?

It *was* a map, floating in the darkness. It appeared lit from within. It was the sort of *living* map he had seen before in Droon. Clouds and birds and the black waves of the Serpent Sea moved across its surface.

There was something else, too. Over the Dark Lands swirled a small purple cloud. As Eric watched, the cloud grew and grew until it finally engulfed all of Droon.

"What is that?" he asked.

The figure beckoned him closer. "You will know soon. For now, speak to me of Droon. Tell me everything. I must know!"

Eric didn't know who the figure was, or what it wanted, but he felt compelled to answer, as if he was under a spell.

"Julie and Neal and I go down the magic stairs in my basement all the time," he began. "Along with Princess Keeah, the wizard Galen, and Max the spider troll, we use our powers to battle the leader of the beasts, Emperor Ko, and his moon dragon, Gethwing."

The green smoke reached at him like a hand, squeezing him, making him go on.

"Then there's Lord Sparr. Everybody knows how evil he used to be. But one of his spells backfired, and he turned into a boy. He helped us a lot. After that, he became himself again. But he was different."

"Different?"

"Sparr tricked Ko," Eric said. "Then he escaped to a strange island where he jumped into a bottomless pit. Now he's gone —"

"Gone! *That's* what I needed to know!"

The scent of apples seemed to engulf Eric suddenly, then oozed back into the darkness.

"Wait!" he said. "Who are you? What's that purple cloud — ?"

"A warning and a challenge for all wizards," the figure said. "Are you up to it?"

"Warning? Challenge? Wait —"

The figure seemed to step away, and the smoky light began to fade. The apple smell drifted away, too. The tunnel grew lighter.

"Wait! Stop!" Eric insisted. "You had me under a spell. You're planning something. Well, you won't get away with it! Neal's a genie and Julie can fly and I'm a wizard with visions and really powerful powers —"

He heard sudden wild chattering all around him and felt his fingertips grow warm.

A hand grasped his shoulder from behind and another from the side.

"Get your beasts off me!" he cried, wiggling free. His fingers sparked wildly, and a beam of silver light exploded into the darkness.

BLAMMMM!

When the smoke cleared, Eric found that the mysterious figure had vanished entirely. Staring at him, her eyes the size of moons, was none other than his teacher, Mrs. Michaels. The hand on his shoulder didn't belong to a beast, but to Neal. The voice in his ear was only Julie's, and the chattering came from his classmates. Finally, the map in front of him wasn't of Droon but of the regular world, and there was a big black hole in its center from the fiery blast he'd sent at it.

He *was* in school, after all.

"Uh-oh," Eric whispered.

Mrs. Michaels stared from Eric's sparking fingers to the map behind her and back again.

"Eric, did you blow up our map?"

His chest pounding, Eric realized he must have just had a vision. Someone

wanted to know about Droon. About Sparr. And whoever he or she was, they were also trying to warn him about something.

Mrs. Michaels moved down the aisle. "What is a Gethwing? And who is Keeah?"

"Dude," Neal hissed in his ear, "you told her everything, totally out loud!"

"Way to spill our secrets, Eric!" added Julie.

"And who is this Lord Spore person —"

"Sparr," said Eric. "I mean . . . who?"

Mrs. Michaels stopped at his desk. "What is this place *Droon* you talked so much about?"

He tried to smile. "Uh . . . well . . . about that . . . you see . . . the thing is . . . could you please repeat the question?"

"No way!" said a girl jumping up from her seat. "Droon is some kind of magical world! I always *knew* there were magical worlds, and this proves it. Let's go to Eric's house now. Can we, Mrs. Michaels? Field trip —"

All of a sudden the door flew open — *bang!* — and a tall man in a cloak of midnight blue and a cone-shaped hat walked into the room.

Backward.

"It's that wizard Eric blabbed about!" cried a boy. "It's Lagen!"

Eric, Julie, and Neal gasped. They knew it wasn't Lagen, or even Galen, the wizard's real name. It wasn't even a real wizard. It was Galen's opposite, the "pretend wizard."

It was Nelag!

Nelag didn't have real powers. He often said and did the exact opposite of what you'd expect. He spoke in riddles, almost never got hurt, and was almost always funny.

"Good-bye, everyone!" said Nelag. "My name is not Nelag!"

Neal groaned. "And I thought it was bad when Eric told everyone we had powers. What is he *doing* here?"

Unrolling a little scroll with tassels hanging from each end, the pretend wizard cleared his throat, lifted four fingers, and said, "I have come for two reasons. First of all, the second reason is . . . Eric, Julie, Neal, I bring a secret message for you! We must go down the secret staircase in Eric's basement. Another secret adventure awaits you secretly in Droon!"

For a moment, silence fell over the classroom. Then everyone exploded.

"Let's go down those magic stairs!"

"There's a shortcut through my yard!"

"This could be extra credit!"

"Wait!" said Mrs. Michaels, facing Nelag. "You said there were *two* reasons. What's the first reason?"

Nelag looked at his four fingers. "I'm so

glad you asked." He stuck those fingers into his mouth and whistled as if he were trying to stop a truck. A tiny yellow bird shot out of the tip of his tall hat, flew to the ceiling, and sprinkled glittery dust over the class.

Everyone fell into a trance.

Mrs. Michaels blinked as the dust fell into her eyes. She spun around, went to the front of the class, turned, and stared into space.

"Eric, Julie, and Neal are dismissed!" she announced. "Everyone else is having a quiz. In science. And English. And social studies. And art. And recess . . ."

"And math?" asked Neal.

"Math, too," said the teacher.

"Whew!" said Neal. "I'm glad I'm missing that one —"

"Neal!" said Julie, pulling him into the hall with Eric and Nelag. "Let's get out of here before they all remember what just happened!"

The four friends shot down the hall. In no time, they were out the door and tearing across the parking lot toward Eric's house.

"That was so nuts!" said Neal. "Eric, what was in your head? You spilled all our secrets!"

"Until Nelag unspilled them," said Julie. "Thanks, Nelag. You were awesome."

Nelag bowed. "I'm told that a lot."

Eric led them across several streets and finally into his yard. "I was having a vision. I was in a very strange lair. Someone made me tell them all about Sparr."

He paused on his back steps and remembered the growing purple cloud. "Guys, the person warned me and said that we'd be challenged today. I think Droon is going to be very weird. We need to be ready."

"Nelag, is that why you came for us?" asked Julie.

Nelag held up four fingers again. "Sorry. I only had two things to tell you. For the rest, we have to go to Droon!"

Eric slipped through his back door, stepped into the kitchen, and listened. "All clear."

The four friends dashed straight to the basement. They pulled a stack of boxes away from a door underneath the stairs and entered a small closet. Nelag stepped in backward.

With a quick *click*, Julie turned off the light. The closet went dark for an instant, then blazed in a glow of rainbow light. A long curving staircase shone brilliantly below.

"What would our friends do if they knew that Droon really *was* real?" asked Neal.

"Same thing I do every time the stairs appear," said Julie. "Freak *out!*"

Laughing despite his uneasiness, Eric took the first step down the stairs, then another and another. Together he and his friends descended through the clouds. They soon saw the silvery walls and colored domes of Jaffa City, the seaside capital of Droon.

Neal tugged a small square of blue cloth from his pocket. When it blossomed into a large, puffy turban, he slipped it on. "Zabilac, First Genie of the Dove, makes an official declaration — adventure, here we come!"

"Except that adventure seems to be coming for us," said Nelag. "Here's some water."

They turned to see a giant black wave barreling across the sea straight toward the city.

"That's not *some* water!" said Eric. "That's all of it! That wave is a hundred feet tall!"

"And it's coming right for us!" yelled Julie.

"It's a wave of death!" Neal cried. "Run!"

"I have a better idea!" said Nelag. "Let's hum! *Brum-dum-de-dum*, a wizard's life for me —" He sat down abruptly on the stairs.

Tripping over him in a mad heap, the children plummeted from the stairs just as the giant wave crashed down.

Two

In the Stone Tree

The four friends tumbled onto the seawall.

"Help!" they cried. "Helpppppp —"

Even before they finished yelling, a man wearing a long blue cloak and carrying a tall staff raced across the plaza below. At his heels ran a girl with flowing blond hair.

"It's Galen!" yelled Neal. "And Keeah!"

"Hold on!" called Galen.

"Hold on?" cried Julie. "To *what*?"

Galen grabbed Keeah's hand, thrust his staff in the ground, and — *floomp!* — the two wizards vaulted to the top of the sea-wall together. While Keeah murmured strange words, Galen took a tiny blue bottle from under his cloak and uncorked it.

"And . . . *in!*" he boomed.

With a tremendous noise and a terrifying wind, the entire wave was sucked right down into the mouth of the tiny bottle!

SLOOOOOORRRRRRP!

In less time than it takes to say it, the wave was gone, the sea was peaceful, and the sun was shining.

"There. That's better!" said Galen. He recorked the bottle and slipped it back in his cloak. "Up now, children. You're fine."

The three friends and Nelag staggered wobbily to their feet.

"What just happened?" asked Neal. "Something magical, I bet."

"Magical, indeed," said Galen. "Much is happening in Droon today, my friends!"

"In our world, too," said Eric. "I had a really strange vision in class this morning. Some stuff I didn't understand."

Galen's face grew serious. "Good. Visions will help us. Come to my tower. Hurry, all!"

The wizard's tower was a tree so old it had long since turned to stone. As they made their way to it, Keeah explained the giant wave and why Nelag was sent to fetch them.

"No sooner had we left the island where Sparr vanished than the island itself vanished into the sea. This caused big waves all over Droon. Galen and I have been busy stopping them. Luckily, this was the last."

Together, the friends entered the tower and started for the top.

"But good has come from the waves, also," added Galen. "They swept Ko and his beasts to faraway shores and scattered Gethwing and his wingsnakes, too."

"My mother and father and their navy were stranded far inland," said Keeah.

"Are they all right?" asked Julie when they reached the tower door.

"Safe and sound!" chirped Max, opening the door and welcoming the children.

Galen's chamber was crammed with books and scrolls, weapons, a giant gold spyglass, statues, mirrors, and half a dozen chairs centered around a workshop table.

Nelag plopped down in front of the telescope and began to yawn.

"We're going to search for the king and queen now," said Max. "We'll journey to an ancient region of Droon called Jabar-Loo!"

"Jabar-Loo. It sounds cool," said Eric.

The princess smiled. "It will be cool. But dangerous, too. I've been reading the ancient scrolls about Droon's early times, to learn as much as I can before we get there."

"Kind of like extra credit!" said Julie.

Neal frowned. "A kid said that same thing in class this morning. What's extra credit?"

"Something we should all be doing all the time," said Galen. "Now, Eric, your vision."

Taking a deep breath, Eric told them everything he could remember about the strange figure in the tunnel. "The person said wizards would be challenged today. Plus, it showed me a purple cloud. It grew and grew until it covered the whole world."

"Use the spyglass!" said Max. "See what you can see."

Leaning over a sleepy Nelag, Eric looked toward the east. All he could see were the black smoky skies of the Dark Lands. "Maybe it isn't big enough yet," he said.

Galen stroked his beard thoughtfully. "Keeah, perhaps it's time for some different extra credit. The red book, I think. The chapter on clouds."

The princess ran over to Galen's bookshelf and pulled a large red book from it. She began leafing through it.

All at once, a tiny light shot in through the tower window and circled their heads.

"Oh my gosh, it's Flink," said Julie. Flink was Galen's pixielike messenger.

The old wizard raised his palm, and the twinkling light settled into it.

"The great white tower of Zorfendorf Castle is gone!" the creature sang.

"What?" said Neal. "Gone? How can a big thing like that just be *gone*?"

"The standing stones of the Ring of Giants, too!" sang Flink. "Even the cobbled wall of Doobesh. Stones from all across Droon are disappearing!"

Galen was aghast. "*Magical* stones are disappearing. There must be a reason. . . . The purple cloud! Eric, this is your vision's warning —"

Suddenly, Keeah jumped, holding the red book in her hands. "I've found it! The cloud is called the Purple Dawn. It happens after a break in time."

"A break in time?" asked Neal.

"A rift," said Galen. "Of course. What we have here is a pathway from Droon's past."

Keeah tapped the page. "Portentia was around for the first Purple Dawn. I say we go to her and ask her what she remembers."

Portentia was an oracle who lived in a

big rock in the Farne Woods near Jaffa City. She spoke in riddles and rhymes and had helped the children many times before.

Galen smiled. "Very good, Keeah. We'll journey for your parents soon, indeed. But this morning's dawn brings more pressing concerns. And I think *you* should be in charge today. What do you say?"

Keeah nodded happily. "I'd love to! Eric, Neal, Julie, everyone — let's hold on tight. We're all going for a ride!"

The princess murmured soft words, and Galen's magical tower began to spin around and around. A minute later, it lifted up from the ground, and the company of friends flew north across the plains toward the Farne Woods.

Three

Stopping by the Woods

Whoosh-shoosh! The flying tower spun over the plains north of Jaffa City and was soon in sight of the dense forest.

"I haven't been to these woods in so long," said Keeah as the tower began its descent. "I can't wait to see Portentia again."

Eric couldn't wait, either. He knew —

as they all did — that Portentia's wisdom about Droon was mystical and deep. If anyone knew about visions, it would be her. "I'm going to ask who came to me in my vision —"

"Wait . . . look!" said Julie. "Something's moving down there!"

Gray and blue feathers flashed across the ground among the lower trees. Then there came another flash of feathers and another.

"Feathers? In the woods?" giggled Nelag. "Well, that's just as it should be. . . ."

"Which means it is *not* as it should be!" said Galen. "I have a fear. Hold on tight. We land!"

The wizard brought the tower down with a resounding *thump*. When everyone rushed out, they found the oracle's lovely grove strewn with broken branches. The place where Portentia normally sat was an empty hole.

"Holy cow!" said Neal. "Maybe she took a walk?"

"She has been stolen!" whispered Galen. He unsheathed his staff and held up his hand.

All was still for a moment — until something fluttered among the trees behind them.

They spun around. A twig snapped. A whistle pierced the air. Then a voice spoke.

"Yoo-hoo, friends! Up here! I'm baaa-ack!"

Perched on a branch high up in an oak tree was an odd creature. From the waist up, it was all black feathers, sharp talons, piercing eyes, and giant beak. From the waist down, it wore a scabbard, leggings, and colorful sandals.

It was none other than Prince Ving, the sweet-talking ruler of the terrible hawk bandits.

"You!" Galen snarled, gripping his staff firmly. "So it's you who has conjured the Purple Dawn to come to the present! Well, take a good look around. You won't be here long enough to enjoy it!"

"Nice to see you, too," said the hawkman.

Ving lived in the past, but the children knew him from the time he had conjured the ancient city of Tarkoom into the present.

"But seriously, folks," he said, his voice calm and quiet. "I just couldn't wait to see you all again. It's so *wonderful* to be here!"

Like Nelag, Ving never said what he really meant. Though his words sounded friendly, the children knew that his meaning was

quite the opposite. Unlike Nelag, though, Ving had only bad things on his mind.

Wings fluttered suddenly and branches cracked, and a flock of bandits leaped up through the trees, carrying a giant net of chains. Caught in the net was Portentia herself.

"Help, friends!" she called. "I'm stolen from my home! And rocks aren't made to roll or roam!"

Galen stepped forward. "Unclaw her, you flying fiends, or I'll —"

"Tut, tut," said Ving. "We are blustery today, aren't we? Besides, we like your talking stone. In fact, I predict we'll have a regular *crush* on her very soon. Icthos! Let's make our friends . . . *comfortable!*"

A branch cracked and there stood Ving's captain, Icthos. His wings were disheveled, his leggings were loose, his sandals tattered, and his eyes wild.

"At yer service, Prince Ving," he said. "We'll feather their beds! Hawks, come!!"

At his call, no less than fifty feathery creatures dived out of the trees. The children backed up. Max trembled. Nelag yawned.

Galen turned to Keeah. "Princess, you are in command today. Anything to suggest?"

Keeah gulped. "Well, there's one thing," she said, raising her fingers. "How about a good old spark fight?"

"Good choice!" said Galen. "Eric, care to join us?"

"My pleasure!" he said.

Before the bandits had time to react, Galen, Keeah, and Eric sprayed the clearing with sizzling sparks. The bandits yelped in surprise.

Eric's fingers grew warm for a second blast when he heard Max cry out — "Eric, behind you!"— and he was tackled from behind by a pair of hawkmen. They flew him up into a tree and left him marooned in the branches.

"Hey!" he yelled. "Not fair!"

Below, the battle wasn't going well for his friends. While Keeah and Galen tried to stop the hawk creatures, the bandits proved to be swift and wily targets. They leaped, dodged, and fluttered clear of every blast.

Icthos let out a battle cry, then jumped directly at Max, swiping his claws wildly. He forced the spider troll back into Nelag and sent them both tumbling over a fallen tree trunk.

Meanwhile, Ving dived at Galen, tripped him up, then swooped at Keeah. "Princess! Nice hairdo today. Are those shoes new?"

"Stop your friendly talk, you fooling fiend!" she snarled. "We know the real you!"

But Ving was quick. He pushed Keeah into Neal and Julie, tangling all three of them in a thicket of briars and thorny vines.

"Sorry to steal and run," the bandit prince crowed. "But we're on a tight deadline. Hawks, now! The big job is still to come!"

With a roar of wings, the whole troop of bandits took to the skies.

"After them!" yelled Galen, charging back toward his tower.

But before they could get close, there came an awful *crunch*, and the tower began to wobble. That's when they saw a crew of bandits flying a chunk of Galen's tower into the sky.

"Thieves! Stealers!" cried Max. "You dare attack the wizard's magic home?"

Ving just laughed. "Toodle-oo, friends!"

The tower teetered and tottered. Then it began to fall.

"I'll stop it!" cried Neal. In a flash, he

was gone. In another flash, he was back, out of breath, his turban nearly undone. The tower was now hanging motionless by several thick ropes tied to the tops of the surrounding trees.

Julie blinked. "What just happened?"

Neal grinned. "Simple. Genies travel in time. I went into the future to when Keeah learned a really cool spell to conjure magical ropes. Then I went into the past and tied up the tower before it hit the ground."

"Well done, Zabilac," said Galen. "But now we see how clever Ving is. While we have been busy with this, he and his bandits have taken Portentia far away. And we still do not know where —"

"Ahem!" said Nelag, raising his hand.

Everyone looked at the pretend wizard.

"I know where they are going," he said.

"I understood that hawky fellow perfectly. Ving said the bandits will have a *crush* on Portentia. Thus, they can be taking her only one place. Where magical stones are crushed to dust. To the stone mills of Feshu."

Galen drew in a long breath. "Feshu!"

The children had first heard of Feshu from Gryndal, the king of the hog elves. When Sparr was his former evil self, he had imprisoned the pig-nosed elves in the stone mills and forced them to work there for a full year before his curse faded.

Galen turned to Keeah. "Well? What do you think? How shall we get there?"

Keeah blinked. "You want me to try this?"

"Even in the midst of trouble, your lessons cannot stop," the wizard said with a smile. "You never know when there will be a quiz."

Neal wagged his head. "Some things

don't change no matter *what* world you're in."

Keeah frowned for a second, then nodded to herself. "Okay. But this is a big one."

Taking a deep breath, she made what seemed almost like animal noises. When she finished, something that sounded halfway between a purr and a whinny came from the trees. Suddenly, five blue-furred animals scampered through the woods to them.

Julie smiled. "Blue pilkas! Our rides!"

The children had ridden blue pilkas once before. The six-legged beasts could not only run very fast, they could also fly.

A sixth pilka trotted in backward, tail first.

"That one's not mine!" said Nelag, leaping straight onto its back. When he landed, he was sitting backward on the backward pilka, so he actually faced forward over its head.

"I have no idea where Feshu is," Nelag said. "So follow me!" He nudged the pilka and it took off, galloping through the woods.

Giving one another looks, the small band mounted the other pilkas — Max sharing Galen's ride — and raced after Nelag. They headed out of the woods and flew up across the plains toward the Dark Lands.

And the growing purple cloud.

Four

Dark Land of Dark Deeds

While their magical blue pilkas soared high over the plains of Droon, the children's gaze was fixed on the faraway horizon. Before long, they saw a faint purple fog moving in the air.

"There it is!" said Max. "Right over Feshu!"

"The thought of those bandits stealing Droon's magical stones fills me with dread," Galen called to the others. "I only hope we arrive in time. A challenge indeed. Ving is dangerous and clever. Let us be clever, too."

"What about dangerous?" asked Neal.

Nelag laughed. "We're *in* danger, for sure. Look!" He pointed down to where flaming arrows were flying at them like a swarm of bees.

Fwing-fwing-fwing!

A troop of red warriors was firing from a hilltop below.

"Ninns!" said Keeah. "We should dive and stop them —"

"Are you sure?" asked Galen, sounding very much like a teacher. "We have a mission. It may not include Ninns."

"I guess you're right," said the princess. "Pilkas, away!"

But no sooner had the pilkas veered from the hilltop than there came a sudden shout. "Wizards, no! Do not leave. Help us!"

Eric tugged his reins. "They sound like they're in trouble. We don't refuse calls for help, do we?"

Galen smiled. "Good answer, Eric. We never refuse anyone help. Let us descend."

Driving their magical creatures downward, the friends soon landed on the hilltop. Lord Sparr's former warriors rushed over.

"Apologies," said the captain, removing his black helmet. "We're sorry for firing at you. We thought you were enemies. We couldn't see clearly. Our eyes are too misted by tears."

"Our minds are misted, too," said a second Ninn. "Because we're so hungry."

"And sad!" added a third.

The children knew that the big warriors had long been evil fighters. But now that Sparr was gone, their tribes wandered aimlessly across the length and breadth of Droon. When they were not forced to fight,

Ninns were often gentle, though sometimes as hard to understand as Nelag.

"Tell us what happened," said Keeah.

The Ninn captain wiped his nose on his sleeve. "We were in our ships, searching for Sparr and his two-headed dog, Kem," he began. "But now all we have are big tears. And each one was stolen!"

"Your tears were stolen?" asked Max.

"Our ships!" said a third, lowering his bow to his side. "They're called the *Nono*, the *Pintsize*, and the *Sink-No-More-Really*."

The children shared a quizzical look.

"Sounds familiar somehow," said Julie.

The captain frowned. "You've had something stolen, too?"

Julie shook her head. "No, I mean —"

"Ahem! Excuse me, I shall question them!" said Nelag. He turned away from the Ninns. "So, who exactly stole your ships?"

"Pirates!" said the Ninn captain. He pulled something long and soft and red from his belt and held it up.

Galen took the object. "A feather? A *hawk* feather? It can't be. . . ."

"When did they come?" asked Nelag.

"While we ate our potatoes," said the captain. "Tasty ones. They had giant wings!"

Neal blinked. "The potatoes had wings?"

"We peeled them first, of course," said the second, scanning the rolling black waves. "They came out of the clouds. With butter!"

"And how many were there?" asked Nelag.

"Two against each of us!" said the third. "Plus one carrot. And a dash of salt."

"They splashed when they struck the water," added a fourth. "They were nice and clean before we cooked them."

"Each one had very sharp claws," said still another. "Sometimes we eat them raw."

"They really scared us," said the captain. "Just thinking about them makes me hungry."

"We gobbled up what we could," agreed another. "Then they flew away into the purple cloud. But we still have room!"

The children stared openmouthed during this whole conversation.

"I understand perfectly," said Nelag. "The Ninns were having a lunch of carrots and potatoes when hawk creatures from the purple cloud dived into the water and surprised them, stealing their ships. The potatoes were nice with butter and salt. The hawks were not."

Galen's face turned paler and paler.

"Hawks at sea?" he said. "Ha! Impossible! The hawk bandits hate water. They never go near it. They have always been land bandits. They are not — *not!* — pirates."

"Master —" said Max.

"Do not say it!" said Galen, scowling.

"Master," said the spider troll softly. "Could it possibly be . . . you-know-who?"

"Pah!" Galen turned away, muttering.

Keeah stamped her foot. "All right, you two, what is going on?"

Max made as if to zip his lips closed, while Galen stared at the sea, grumbling.

Finally, the wizard sighed and spoke. "The hawk bandits of Prince Ving do not fly over water or swim. They never have and they never will. They hate water in all its forms. But . . . there *are* hawk creatures who love the water."

"Hawk pirates, in fact," said Max.

"Pirates?" asked Eric.

"Arrrh!" said Nelag. "Ving has a twin!"

The children were stunned.

"A twin?" said Neal. "You mean there are two of him? Is he as nasty and ruthless and nutty and mean and dangerous and mean as Ving is? Is he?"

Max sighed. "Ving's twin is not a he."

"He's a . . . *she*?" said Keeah.

Galen's face turned white. "She is a trickster of the most evil sort. Her name is Ming. A long time ago, Ving and Ming divided their territory. Ving's bandits stole on land, and Ming took to the sea with her pirates. He became the bandit prince and she the pirate princess."

"The pirate princess," whispered Julie.

"She tricked Galen once," said Nelag with a smile. "Boy, that was something!"

"Nelag!" said the wizard angrily. "You have been told never to mention that!"

Eric glanced at Keeah and his friends. He knew they were all wondering the same thing he was. *How had Ming tricked the wizard? Why wouldn't he talk about it?*

"But listen here," said Galen. "The twins dislike each other. Only the most sinister reason can explain them working together —"

The Ninn captain pointed suddenly to the horizon. "Our ships! The *Nono*! The *Pintsize*!"

As they watched, the first two of the three Ninn ships sailed into view. Their usual red flags had been torn away and replaced by banners the color of the dawn.

When the masts of the third and largest vessel edged over the horizon, Nelag frowned. "Here come the presents. But I don't think they are for us."

Lying across the deck of the third ship were giant white stones. They looked like long, curved columns that came to a point.

They were, in fact, big stone tusks stolen from the Horns of Ko, the giant crushing rocks named after the beast leader.

"Holy cow," said Eric. "Stealing from Ko. They don't even care if the emperor gets mad. Why are they stealing all these stones?"

"We know one thing," said Keeah. "The pirates are sailing those ships to Feshu."

The Ninn warrior's broad red face drained of color. "Feshu. That is a place of dark doings."

"We know," said Julie. "That's why we're going there. To stop the hawk bandits — and pirates — from doing whatever they're doing!"

The Ninn nodded firmly. "Then we will go to Feshu, too. We need our ships to keep searching."

"For Sparr?" asked Keeah.

"And potatoes," said the second Ninn.

"We miss them. Especially his little doggie, Kem."

"I understand completely," said Nelag.

As the Ninns started their long march along the coast to Feshu, the pilka fliers continued their journey high across Droon.

Hours passed until the purple cloud was overhead. And there below it stood a vast hulk of chimneys and towers. In its center was an enormous black iron wheel.

"The Feshu stone mills," said Galen. "The sight I was dreading."

No sooner had the pilkas landed unseen behind a rise in the land when there came a terrible roar like thunder — *foooom!* — and a shriek of iron against stone — *kreeeee!* — and the terrifying black wheel began to turn.

Five

The Crushing Wheel

When the small band crept over the hill and looked down, Julie gasped. "How horrible!"

It *was* horrible. The mill wheel was a thick, iron disk that must have stood a hundred feet high. Ranged all along its edge were fierce, jagged gears. When the wheel turned, it made the most terrifying sound.

The children knew why. With every movement of the wheel and every smoky belch from the chimneys, stones were being crushed and ground to dust.

"Stones are stones, but magical ones are different," said Galen softly. "If it takes the rest of my days, I will find a charm to reverse this destruction."

"I'll help," said Keeah.

"We all will," added Neal.

Max shivered as he scanned the vast millworks. "The Ninns are not the only ones afraid of this place," he chirped. "The hog elves knew the terror of it. Poor Gryndal was trapped here with his friends for a full year."

As the small group watched, the mills grew shrouded in a haze of swirling ash. Down below, armed bandits patrolled a big open yard of stolen rocks and stones. There were broken columns, cob- blestones, walls, and every manner of stone stacked high.

In the center sat a plump rock they knew well. It was Portentia.

A shout from the shore called most of the bandits from the yard. They flew down to help unload the approaching ships.

"How nice, look!" said Nelag, pointing.

A half-dozen bandits stayed behind to hoist Portentia into a wagon. They rolled it toward a wide door in the mill.

Eric smiled. "Nice is right. We can follow Portentia into the mill before the gate closes."

"Keeah, everyone," said Galen, "today has already seen our challenges begin. Let us hope we are up to all of them. First we must save Portentia. Then we stop Ving and Ming. That's our mission, short and sweet. Come!"

After securing their pilkas, the little band dashed over the rise and ran into the yard. They hid where they could, then crept through the mill's gate at the last possible moment. By the time the door slammed shut, the seven friends were crouched in the shadows of a narrow passage.

They heard the creaking wheels of the wagon, the stomping of the bandits' heavy feet, and the moaning of Portentia echoing from the halls. But the moment they stepped down the passage, they found that the mill was a maze of twisting hallways and tight passages, steep ramps and abrupt dead ends.

When several passages crisscrossed one another at wild angles, the little band stopped completely.

Julie groaned softly. "I can't believe we already lost Portentia. This place is *so* crazy."

"To confuse unwanted visitors, no doubt," said Galen. He peered into a passage lit by a single wall torch, then turned. "Keeah, as our leader today, what do *you* think we should do?"

The princess frowned into the gloom, then at her friends. She shrugged. "Split up?"

Galen nodded. "Exactly what I would have said. If I may choose sides, Nelag and I shall follow the left hall. My staff will light our way."

"Max and I can take the middle passage," said Julie. "It's not too dark."

"Eric, Neal — we'll follow the light," said Keeah. "Above all, let's find Portentia!"

With a nod, Galen disappeared down the side hall, with Nelag trailing behind him.

Julie and Max entered the passage in the middle.

Keeah took a deep breath. "Guys, let's go."

With every step forward, their hearts beat faster. Since the tunnel was low, both

Neal and Eric had to duck when they passed under the torch. The moment they did, the passage twisted and turned. But just when darkness fell again, another torch lit their way.

"Nice of them to give us light," said Keeah.

"Uh-huh," said Eric, pausing under the next torch. "Except unless there are five identical torches lighting five identical passages, I think we're going in circles."

"Are you serious?" said Neal. "Should we go back?"

"Or would that be part of the circle?" asked Keeah.

Eric kept staring at the light. "And did anyone notice how the flames aren't that hot? They're not even warm —"

All of a sudden, the fire flared wildly, then dripped off the torch and settled on the floor.

"Whoa!" gasped Neal, jumping back.

The "flames" sat on the stones, three slender ribbons of silver, each with a tiny upturned head.

"Silfs!" Keeah exclaimed. "They're silfs!"

Silfs were snaky underwater creatures loyal to the Sea Witch, Keeah's aunt Demither. When the silvery creatures wanted to hide, they often disguised themselves as flames.

The three creatures bowed to Keeah. "Princess-s-s-s!" the first one hissed. "It's good to s-s-see you . . . only not here!"

"What are you doing in the stone mills so far from your undersea home?" Keeah asked.

"The pirates-s-s captured us-s-s," the silf replied. "To tell them s-s-s-something."

"But we es-s-s-scaped before they could ask us-s-s-s-s," said the second.

"We are quite s-s-s-slippery, after all,"

said the third. "Besides, we cannot lie. We mus-st tell the truth, no matter *who* asks-s-s us-s-s. To keep from telling any s-s-secrets-s, we hid!"

The three friends looked at one another.

"Maybe the hawks think that the secret is in the water," said Eric.

"Good one," said Keeah. "And that's why Ming is here. She can go in the water and Ving can't. Or doesn't want to."

Eric nodded. "That makes sense."

"Have you seen Portentia?" asked Neal. "She rhymes and tells the future. Plus, she's a rock."

"The hawks-s-s took her to the dungeon with all the other magical stones-s-s," the third silf said. "When we s-saw her, she was trying to find a rhyme for . . . *bandit.* This-s-s way!"

Keeah nodded. "Let's go."

The three friends crept after the silvery

snakes. Into tunnels, up ramps, and down stairs they went until they found a passage so dark that not even the silfs could light it up.

"We are near," said one of them.

All at once, they heard murmuring from somewhere in the darkness. Stepping ahead, they realized it was a voice they knew.

"Oh, I'm not free," it said. "But that's not all. For soon I'll be a great big wall!"

"It's Portentia!" whispered Keeah.

The three friends and three silfs found the large stone sitting in a great room. Thick chains held her down. She was rocking back and forth, struggling to free herself.

"Portentia, we've found you!" said Eric.

"Oh, dears!" she said. "I just can't stand it! Chained up by that dreadful bandit!"

"Good rhyme," said Neal. "You really know your words."

"How's this for rhyming *words*?"

snapped a voice from the shadows. "You've just been captured by hawk-winged *birds*!"

"That's pretty good, too," said Neal. "Hey, wait —"

They didn't wait.

Amid a blaze of real torchlight, bandits sprang out of every crevice and nook in the chamber and seized the children tightly. There were dozens of hawk creatures dressed in the ragged uniforms of bandits, all staring with menacing eyes at the captives.

And there, not far away, chained so tightly they couldn't budge, were Julie and Max. Next to them, his face grim and dark, was Galen himself.

"Holy crow," cried Neal. "We've *all* been captured!"

It was impossible to fight. Eric, Keeah, and Neal were quickly bound with chains like the others. Then, in a loud flourish of flapping wings, two figures appeared in the chamber.

Ving swaggered in, wearing a long purple cloak, his dark feathers blazing, his claws gleaming in the torchlight. "Hi, folks!"

Next to him, with wings as red as the setting sun, her beak as shiny as ebony, her eye patch trimmed with diamonds, was none other than Ming herself.

With a rustle of feathers and a breathy whisper, the pirate princess spoke.

"At last. All our guests have arrived!"

Six

Double Your Fun!

The dungeon sparked with electricity when Ming stepped over to Galen.

"You!" snarled the wizard, glaring into her single eye.

"And you!" Ming laughed brightly. "We meet again, dear wizard."

Even though he struggled, there was nothing Galen could do. Bandits and pirates continued to crowd the chamber until there was barely room to move. Eric realized that the only way to really tell them apart was that the pirates wore eye patches and earrings, carried cutlasses, and mumbled "Arrrh," while the bandits had clubs in their belts, satchels over their shoulders, and eyed the children silently.

Ming glared at the captives. "You all look so mopey. Maybe this will cheer you up. Ving? The plans!"

"What about them?" asked Ving.

"Bring them!" she said.

"Why me? Why not you?" he said.

"Because I'm older than you!" she said.

"By twenty seconds!"

"Oh, just do it!" Ming squealed.

Her twin brother muttered to himself. He snapped his claws, and several bandits pushed their way through the crowd. They carried rolled-up blueprints, sketches, and something under a purple cloth. They set these on top of a flat gray stone that the children recognized as having come from the Ring of Giants.

Ving removed the purple cloth. "Ta-da!"

Underneath the cloth stood the model of a vast city. It had walls of gold with jagged spikes ranged around the top. Many towers stood inside the walls. The summits of the towers were shaped like hawk heads, with razor-sharp beaks and black eyes staring menacingly in all directions.

"What's that terrible place?" asked Julie.

"The city of Mokarto," said Ving.

"Remind me never to visit," said Neal.

"Where is it?" asked Galen.

"Nowhere, yet," said Ming. "But it'll soon stand right here in Feshu. With the help of these stone mills. And your princess here —"

"Me?" Keeah asked.

"We've gathered all the magical stones

we need for our magical city," said Ving. "There is only one thing more we need. And you, Princess, will tell us where to find it!"

"Fat chance," snapped Keeah. "Besides, I don't know what you're talking about."

It was then Eric realized that the silfs must have escaped again, for they were nowhere in sight. Not only that, he noticed that someone else was missing, too. He leaned toward Galen.

"Where's Nelag?" he whispered.

Galen sighed. "Lost," he whispered.

Eric understood. Nelag must have gotten lost in the passages. But at least he was free. Maybe he could even help them escape.

A hawk bandit with knobby knees, a large red mustache, and an even larger belt buckle entered the dungeon.

"Your Majesties!" he said. "Come along to the viewing tower. The first stones are coming from the mill. Mokarto is beginning to rise!"

Ving laughed. "All right, then. Everyone to the roof! Let's see our city taking shape!"

The hawk creatures dragged their prisoners from the chamber. Up they went through the passages, floor by floor, until they emerged on the mill's large, flat roof.

The first thing the children saw was that the purple cloud had grown huge. And it had darkened as the afternoon wore on.

"Living in the past is like trying to breathe without air," said Ving, striding across the rooftop. "That's why we conjured the Purple Dawn. Now we're building a magical new home in your world. Behold Mokarto, the terrible city of thieving thieves!"

The friends were shocked at the vastness of the construction going on before them. Hundreds of hawk bandits were busily moving stones. An outer wall stretching for miles was rising course by course. The hawk-headed towers, too, were beginning to take shape. One after another, buildings were going up, and streets were winding around and around, until Mokarto stretched all the way from the plains of Feshu to the coast.

The worst part was that the stones emerging from the mill were nothing like the ancient magical stones that had entered the mill. Now they were smooth and square and bore a deep golden color.

Ving chuckled with glee. "We tried once before to live in your world. We tried to bring Tarkoom back, but you sent us back to the past in a heap. This time, we're building from scratch. And because Mokarto is made of magical stones, it'll be invincible!"

"All we need," said Ming, glaring at Keeah, "is one simple thing. The gate to

Mokarto will open only with the legendary Key of Mokarto. Ring any bells, honey?"

Keeah stared back. "I've never heard of it. How could I know where it is?"

Ming grinned coldly. "The Key of Mokarto is hidden somewhere under the sea. Legends say that Demither showed you where."

"Demither? When?" said Keeah. "I've never heard of the key!"

"Oh, you have," said Ming. "Though you may not remember. But . . . the silfs might. Since you are Demither's niece, they are loyal to you. They will tell us where the key is if they know you are in trouble. Of course, if I must, I'll make you walk the plank to unlock your memory —"

"Too messy," said Ving. "Let's put her in the cage of light instead!"

Before she could move, Keeah was released from her chains and pushed onto a strange pedestal on the roof. Sizzling bars of light shot up around her in a wild criss-crossing pattern, trapping the princess securely inside the cage.

"Why, you —" cried Galen. "I'll not stand for this!" With a single powerful blast, he burst his chains and lunged at the bandits, taking down three of them. Twirling on his heels, he leaped toward the pirates, knocking down five more. He blasted the chains away from the children, then cried, "Keeah, duck!"

He aimed a blast at the cage of light, but Ving flew at him quickly, tackling the wizard. They both tumbled from the roof, while the children ran.

"Pirates, stop them!" shouted Ming. She flew across the rooftop toward them.

Galen had disappeared, but the children didn't get far. A horde of pirates yelling "Arrrh!" stopped them cold.

Snarling in anger, Ming commanded her forces to take the friends down to the darkest room in the deepest level of the mill.

The sad procession tramped lower and lower into the depths of the mill. It was almost half an hour before they reached a big iron door.

"Arrrh! Welcome to the Blast-Proof-Dungeon-That-Can't-Be-Escaped-From. Arrrh!" growled a disheveled pirate. "Ooh, a magic hat!" He grabbed Neal's turban and shut the door with a bang.

For a full five minutes, the kids heard the slamming of ever-more-distant doors.

At last, it was quiet.

"Oh, this is just great!" said Julie. "No Keeah. No Galen. Not even Nelag! There's no way to call Flink and get help. Boy, what I wouldn't give for a small army of hog elves to help us now. Gryndal probably knows these mills backward and forward.

If we could find a way to . . . to . . . oh, what's the use!"

Neal rubbed his head. "I could have gone into the future and found us a way out. But without my turban, I'm just boring old Neal again. Boring old *hungry* Neal."

Max crawled on the ceiling, searching for cracks in the stone. "I do hope Keeah's all right in that dreadful contraption," he said. "If Galen and Nelag can get free, they just might be able to rescue us."

Eric had been vainly searching the walls for a way out when he suddenly froze. "You guys, I just thought of something. Maybe we're not trapped in this dungeon. At least, maybe *I'm* not. I made a phantom of myself once. I split myself in two, and both halves could do stuff. If I do it again, I could get out of this cell. I can free Keeah. We could call Flink. We can get help for all of us —"

Julie frowned. "Wait. Do you have powers as a phantom?"

Eric didn't remember using his powers as a phantom. "I'm not sure. But being half in here and half out there has got to be better than just being in here."

"If I could be in two places at once," said Neal, "I'd want them both to be restaurants. But, you know, whatever."

While the sounds of the construction grew louder, Eric closed his eyes and tried to concentrate. An odd feeling, almost like drifting off to sleep, fell over him.

Then, as one part of him remained in the dungeon with his friends, he sensed another part begin to slip away. Feeling like no more than a ghost of himself, Eric pressed his hands against the wall once more.

And he fell right through it, head over heels, until he lay in the passage outside.

Seven

Helping a Friend

Finding himself in the dim passage just outside the dungeon, Eric looked down at himself. He seemed normal. Two arms, two legs, two hands, two feet.

"Excellent," he said to himself. "I actually did it."

Looking to the right, he could just make out a troop of bandits at one end. When he peered the other way, he nearly screamed in surprise when he saw Galen hiding in the shadows.

"Hush!" hissed the wizard. "Come here." Galen motioned him into the shadows. "I slipped away from Ving — after giving him a taste of my staff! So, are you a phantom?"

Eric nodded. "I'm going to try to free Keeah, call Flink and ask her to get the hog elves, then find a way to shut down the mills before Mokarto is finished being built."

The old wizard smiled deeply. "A tall order, Eric. Today is a day of challenges indeed. I cannot join you just yet. I have one trick up my sleeve, but only one. Ming has a power over me I cannot explain. That is my challenge. Now, be watchful. And remember, not everything is as it seems to be. Think like Nelag. Think opposite!"

With those strange words, Galen was gone.

Eric tried to hold all that in his head,

but it refused to make sense. "Never mind," he told himself. "I have my own mission."

Creeping down the passage, he realized that if he closed his eyes for a second he could see inside the dungeon as if he were still there. When he tried this, he heard Neal talking to him.

"... and if you see something to eat, bring it back here ... I mean, it doesn't even have to be muffins, anything would be great ... just bring lots ..."

"Neal, I've got a job to do!" Eric told him.

"I'm just saying ..."

Shaking his head to clear it, Eric was back outside the dungeon again.

Darting from one passage to the next, always staying clear of the troops of bandits and pirates marching everywhere, Eric finally located a door leading outside. He slipped through it and found himself out on the roof.

Keeah was still trapped in the cage of light. Both Ving and Ming were nearby, talking to each other.

Arguing with each other, Eric thought.

He crept as close to the edge of the parapet as he dared. He knew that even though he was a phantom, he was still visible.

Ving paced across the top of the mill, pausing every few seconds to check his sketches and watch the construction.

"Why else would I invite you, sister?" he said. "You're not my favorite person, you know."

Ming glared coldly at her twin. "And I'd rather be sailing. But Mokarto needs both of us, or it won't exist. And if it doesn't exist, it's back to the past, and I'm tired of the past. The food is so . . . stale!"

"Did someone say 'food'?" asked Neal from the dungeon.

"Quiet. I'm listening!" Eric hissed. He noticed Icthos circling the parapet. The bandit landed on the roof and limped over to Ving and Ming. He was carrying a small brown box.

Eric couldn't see what was inside, but when Ving and his sister opened it, the silvery glow on their faces told him that the silfs had been recaptured.

"Tell me where the Key of Mokarto is!" demanded Ming. "You must tell me the truth. Speak, silfs, or I'll deal harshly with my prisoner!"

"Our prisoner," said Ving.

The hissing that started then was soft, but it soon grew to a great noise, until Ming snapped the box shut and shouted with joy.

"I know where it is! We shall be invincible! Ving, alert my ships. We sail at once!"

"What am I, your servant?" snapped Ving.

His sister grinned. "For this part of our plan, you are. For only I can get the key now!"

"Whatever. Just watch your tone," he muttered.

While the bandit prince flew off, Icthos remained at Keeah's cage.

"Shall I take the princess to the dungeon with the others?" he asked.

Ming glared at Keeah. "No. Let her watch Mokarto's towers rise taller than those of Jaffa City! I'm going sailing!"

With that, the pirate princess cackled and stormed away to her waiting ships.

With only Icthos as guard, Eric moved closer to the cage. He spied the lever that turned the light beams on and off. If he could get to that, he thought, he'd switch it off and Keeah could jump free.

But Icthos was too close for comfort.

"I'll distract him," Eric said to himself. Looking down at his feet, he saw a stone the size of a softball and smiled. "Perfect!"

Keeping his eyes fixed on Icthos, Eric grabbed the stone and hurled it past the bandit's head.

Nothing happened. Icthos scratched his nose and began to sing a little tune. *"Brum-dum-de-dum* . . . a bandit's life for me!"

Grumbling, Eric searched for another stone to throw, when he saw the first one still lying on the roof between his feet.

"Hey, I threw you!" This time, he used both hands to pick it up, only to watch his fingers come together and the stone remain where it was. He swiped at it again and again but couldn't grab it. When he tried other stones, the same thing happened.

He sat back, bewildered, until it came to him. "Of course! I'm not just a phantom.

I must be a kind of *ultra* phantom. The dungeon walls were so thick, the only way I could get out was to make myself almost a nothing. A ghost! I can be seen and I can talk, but I have no powers. I can't lift anything or touch anything or" — he looked over at the cage of light —"or free Keeah!"

The giant grinding wheel began to turn faster. A roar went up from the bandits on the ground, and the terrible city of thieving thieves rose higher.

"This is perfect!" Eric whispered.

He knew he had to do something. If he didn't have powers of his own just then, he needed someone who did. Keeah was their only chance to stop Ming.

He took a deep breath and scampered the rest of the way across the roof until he was directly behind Keeah's cage of light.

"*Psst!*" he said.

Keeah glanced back over her shoulder. "Eric?" she whispered. "Is that you?"

"Sort of," he said.

"Finally, I can get out of here. Switch the lever off while Icthos isn't looking."

"Uh, yeah, about that," he whispered. "The only reason I escaped is because I became a phantom. I mean, I look regular, but I can't move the lever. In fact, I couldn't even pick up a potato chip —"

"*Did you say 'potato chip'?*" asked Neal from the dungeon. "*Are there some where you are?*"

"Neal, please," said Eric. "Keeah, wait. I think I can get Icthos to turn the cage off. I'm going to try something . . ."

Hoping he wouldn't just get zapped to death, Eric held his breath and stepped through the bars of sizzling light and into the cage. Nothing happened.

"Whoa!" he breathed. "That could have

gone so wrong. Okay, Keeah, pretend to hold my hand and let me do the talking."

She made a face at him. "Are you sure you know what you're doing?"

Eric shrugged. "I have to try. Now, *shhh*. Hey, Icky! Your cage doesn't work so well!"

The bandit turned, and his eyes grew huge. "What are *you* doing in there?"

"Nothing, anymore," said Eric. "We're leaving." Giving a little wave, he pretended to pull Keeah's hand with him as he stepped through the bars of light and onto the roof.

"The cage looks like it's on," whispered Eric, "but I'm pretty sure the lever's off. Come on, Kee-Kee, we're out of here!"

"Wait!" shouted the bandit, pulling a nasty-looking club from his belt. "That cage ain't working right. You get back in there!"

While Eric stepped politely back into the cage, Icthos bent to the lever. Using both hands, he turned it the other way.

The instant the light faded, Eric yelled "Now!" And he and Keeah jumped out of the cage and onto the roof.

"Thanks for letting us go!" said Keeah. "Oh, and one more thing!" She snatched the box of silfs and tripped lightly across the roof. "Who says all bandits are bad?!"

"You tricked me!" Icthos yelled. "Come back!"

"Let me think about that. Umm, no!" said Eric.

In seconds, Keeah had conjured a spinning circle of blue light. "Eric, hold tight. Or something. We're going to the pilkas and we're going to find that key!"

Eric couldn't really hold Keeah's hand, but it didn't matter. His phantom self was swept into her tube of spinning blue, and they were off the roof in a twinkling.

They soared high over Feshu and alighted behind the ridge where their pilkas were waiting. Eric wondered if he would be able to ride one. While he struggled to grip the creature's fur and pull himself onto its back, Keeah opened the box.

The silfs began hissing immediately.

"We told Ming everything!" said the first.

"It's-s-s s-somewhere in the Doom Gate of Queen Demither!" said the second.

"Somewhere?" said Keeah. "But the Doom Gate has hundreds of rooms!"

"Only you know where the key is-s-s," said the third. "Demither told you long ago. This-s-s is-s-s all we know!"

Keeah stood perfectly still for a moment, then nodded firmly. "Okay, then. We'll have to search room by room. But we need some help."

"I need some help, too," said Eric, sitting on the ground under his pilka. "I can't stay on."

"We'll help," said the silfs together.

Keeah spoke under her breath, and a twinkly light appeared in the sky overhead.

It was Flink.

"Yes-s-s, Princess-s-s!" she sang.

"Flink, find Gryndal as quickly as you can," said Keeah. "Tell him what's happening at Feshu. The king of the hog elves knows the stone mills better than anyone. We'll meet him as soon as we can. Fly, Flink, fly!"

The tiny messenger sizzled across the air and was gone.

By now, Eric was on his pilka's back, but he knew he would fall if not for the silfs holding him. "I'm ready," he said. "I think."

"That'll have to do," said Keeah. "Now let's go! We have a pirate ship to stop!"

"Okay —" Clinging for dear life, Eric and his pilka rose into the air after Keeah. Together, the two friends soared high over the black waters of the vast Serpent Sea.

Eight

Doom at the Dome

Mile after mile of black water churned below the two pilkas as the children flew toward Demither's sea palace.

"If we don't find the key first, Ming will wreck my aunt's palace looking for it," said Keeah.

"She might not have to do much wrecking," said Eric. "Take a look."

The Sea Witch's once-splendid underwater city was floating derelict on the waves. Demither had been in the Upper World for some time, but the children were still shocked to see the palace now. Only the cracked top of its green dome stood above the water.

"Ohh!" gasped one of the silfs. "It's worse than before! And here comes Ming!"

The pirate ships appeared over the horizon and sailed swiftly toward them.

"Let's get down there now," said Keeah.

Before the pilkas could land, however, the air turned red with flame.

Boom! Boom! The pirates shot the Ninn cannons, hurling fiery blasts right at the diving pilkas. They dodged the first blast. The children clung tight as the pilkas soared up, but a second and third round of cannon fire were already on the way.

"I have to save the pilkas!" cried Keeah.

"But what about us?"

"Sorry! Hold your breath!" Keeah

whispered a phrase and — *poof!* — the pilkas vanished just before the shots struck.

Splash! Splash! The children fell straight into the water, with the silfs by their side. They swam to the dome and climbed up on the far side of it.

When Eric stood on the dome, he realized he wasn't wet. Except for his hand.

"I wonder if that means my real self is coming back."

"We could sure use your powers," said Keeah.

Eric closed his eyes for a second. He couldn't see the dungeon as clearly as before, but he could make out Neal trying to shake hands with his phantom hand.

"This is sooo weird!" Neal was saying.

"Leave Eric alone!" said Julie.

"This-s-s way!" said the silfs.

Together, Eric and Keeah followed the silvery sea snakes through the cracked dome and dropped into Demither's empty throne room. It was half flooded. Watery light quivered on the walls.

The silfs led them quickly across the great room.

"The poor palace," said Keeah. "It's dying."

"Demither will be back," said Eric. "I know it."

Keeah tried to smile. "I hope so —"

A sudden crash of glass hushed them.

"What was that?" Eric whispered.

"The pirates-s-s have broken in," said one silf. "We'll s-stay and try to s-slow them down. You hurry!"

"The Doom Gate is at the bottom of the palace," said Keeah. "Eric, swim down. If you can!" She dived beneath the water and wiggled away under it like a fish.

"I'm coming!" Eric said. Holding his breath, he followed her down through the passages. His hair was wet now, too, and so were his shoulders. *I'm coming back!* he thought. *Soon my powers will return!*

From one floor to another, gasping for air where they could, the two friends made their way to a grotto of coral beneath the palace. It was filled with air.

On the far side of the grotto was a great slab of stone that arched up to the ceiling like a door. A lock carved in the shape of Keeah's hand stood in the center. Long ago, Demither had made her niece the only one who could open the fortified vault.

"The Doom Gate," said Eric. He remembered that he had first received powers there. It seemed like a lifetime ago.

Keeah placed her hand on the imprint. The giant door slid open noiselessly. Water rushed around their feet as the two friends entered.

Together they went from treasure room

to treasure room. Keeah stopped here and there and murmured softly to herself.

"Demither shared her secrets with me, but I don't remember. Everyone says the key is here. I just don't know where. . . ."

While the sounds of pirates yelling and splashing echoed into the Doom Gate from above, Keeah and Eric moved as swiftly as they could. They searched room after room, looking through wands and masks, shiny jewelry and odd weapons, but found no key. They came finally to a single empty room.

Eric glanced in and was about to turn away, when his left leg suddenly became solid. He lost his balance and fell. "Owww!"

Keeah rushed into the room to help him.

"No, don't!" cried Eric. "You'll crush it!"

She stopped cold. "Crush what?"

"That!" He pointed to an object on the floor.

Keeah stepped back and looked down. Nearly invisible in the center of the floor was a tiny white object no bigger than the cap from a soda bottle.

Squinting at it, Eric realized that it was a miniature palace. He tried to pick it up. He couldn't.

"Because you're a phantom," said Keeah, bending to the floor.

"No," he said. "Because . . . it's heavy!"

She tried to move the building, too. "I remember this. Only it was bigger!"

As if her words were charmed, the tiny palace began to grow and grow. It filled the room until it stood there, an enormous play palace built for a princess.

The stale, watery air in the Doom Gate suddenly smelled like a garden.

The palace was completely white with several rooms draped in blue and green and yellow curtains. Keeah walked under the front arch and pulled aside the curtains. Eric followed her. There, among pearl bracelets and necklaces of sea jewels, lay a small golden key with a blue ribbon on it.

Eric felt his heart beat against his chest. "The Key of Mokarto?"

Keeah stared at it for a while, then said, "Long ago, before Demither took me with her to the Upper World, I lived with her in her palace. I remember now. These were my toys. Eric, we found it —"

The stone door shuddered behind them.

"They're right outside!" said Eric.

"They won't get the key," said Keeah, snatching it up. "All we need to do is stay here two hours until sunset. Then it will be too late. Mokarto will never open, and we'll have stopped them —"

There was a soft, hissing sound from outside the Gate. The children put their ears to the door and listened.

"Help us-s-s! The pirate princess-s-s has captured us-s-s!"

Eric felt his heart sink. "She has them. Ming has the silfs."

"S-s-save us-s-s!"

Keeah looked at the key and sighed. "We have no choice," she said. She placed her hand on the inside of the stone door, and it slid aside.

Ming's red feathers glimmered in the watery light. When she snapped her claws, dozens of growling pirates seized the children.

But the silfs were nowhere in sight.

The pirate princess grinned. "S-s-sorry to dec-c-ceive you. The s-silfs escaped long ago into the s-s-sea. But you won't. Unless you give me that key now. Besides, outnumbered much?"

They *were* outnumbered, at least thirty to one. And Eric still didn't have his full powers back. Keeah alone couldn't stop Ming.

The pirate princess snatched the key from her, then gazed around the treasure room. "Pirates, find some chains and bind these troublemakers."

"Arrrh!" The pirates bound the children with silver chains from the first treasure room.

"Now, stay put until we return," said Ming. "I'm going to furnish Mokarto with some of these trinkets. Pirates, come. We sail!"

"Arrrh!" they roared again, and followed their princess from Demither's palace.

But the moment the pirates left, Eric felt the chains binding him slip away. "Hey!"

"S-s-surprise!" said the silfs. "It was the leas-s-st we could do! Now, go. Hurry!"

The two friends raced through the passages, up the floors of the palace from the grotto to the very top of the dome.

The pirate ships were already sailing back to Feshu, their terrible purple banners flying high.

"Should we conjure up those pilkas again?" asked Eric. "We need speed."

Keeah raised her hands, then lowered them again. "I don't think we need them. Look!"

There was a great flash of white in the air above them. Looking up, the children saw Gryndal, the elf king, riding atop a giant four-winged bird called a soarwing. Flink was perched on his shoulder.

Eric jumped. "Powers or no powers, sometimes we're just plain lucky!"

"Jump on," shouted Gryndal.

Laughing, the two friends skittered across the great dome and leaped onto the bird's shimmering back.

"We came as soon as we could!" said Gryndal, banking the bird high over the sea.

"We?" said Keeah.

"Me and my . . . army!"

With a second flash of white, another soarwing flew up next to them. On its back sat dozens and dozens of hog elves. They didn't carry weapons, but they were armored from head to toe. They waved to the children.

"When we saw the pirates' ships, we knew where you were," said Gryndal.

"We have no time to waste," said Eric. "To Feshu! To save our friends! And Droon!"

The two friends and a small army of hog elves swept across the sea and down toward the gloomy stone mills. There, a dreadful sight greeted them. For Mokarto — the terrible city of thieving thieves — was finished!

Nine

Home, Evil Home

Seeing the white birds circling the city, Ving clacked his beak and gave out a shrill whistle.

"Welcome them the bandit way!"

With a flash of feathers and a roar of wings, the hawk army took to the skies.

Diving to avoid the hawk creatures, the children swept over the vast, dark city below.

Whoosh-whoosh-whoosh! Gloom surrounded the fliers as they dipped among
Mokarto's towers and turrets. All at once,
Eric felt the hair on the back of his neck
tingle. He glanced down into a large plaza
and yelped.

"Whoa, look. Look at them!"

Hawk creatures stood silently in forma-
tion as far as the eye could see. Eyes closed,
wings folded, shrouded in the long purple
shadows of afternoon, they were nothing
less than an army waiting to awake.

Gryndal quivered. "Oh, dear me!"

"I can't believe that tiny golden key will
bring all this to life," said Keeah.

"Permanent life," said Gryndal.

"Magically invincible life!" said Eric.

"That door can't be opened!" said Keeah
firmly. "There's just no way. No way!"

On Gryndal's command, the birds

climbed again and soared over Feshu, prepared to battle the bandits once more.

But it was not to be.

Galen was nowhere to be seen, but Max, Neal, and Julie were trapped in front of the Mokarto gate, surrounded by hundreds of bandits and pirates, Icthos, and the hawk twins themselves.

Ming marched up from the shore with her army of pirates. She raised her claws to the flying friends. "The bandits will soon find Galen," she yelled, "but having these three creatures is enough to make you do what we want. Come down, or else."

"She's got us again," Keeah groaned.

"She keeps doing that!" said Eric.

"It's because we have feelings and friends," the princess replied.

Keeah, Gryndal, and Eric landed the giant birds nearby.

"You're just in time for the grand opening of Mokarto," said Ving. "The terrible city of thieving thieves will be open for business! Ming, would you care to do the honors?"

The pirate princess grinned. "I would."

"Oh, this is terrible," said Max. "No, no, you can't do this!"

"Tut-tut," said a voice. "Let her pass!" There was a puff of smoke and a shower of sparks, and Galen appeared among them.

"Galen!" Julie shouted.

"The one and only!" said the wizard. "Let Ming open the gate. Let her!"

"You can't!" cried Keeah, struggling. "There are thousands of terrible creatures in there waiting to wake. They'll overrun Droon!"

"Let her pass," the wizard repeated, laughing to himself.

Her outstretched claw nearly at the lock, Ming paused. She glared at the wizard. "Why aren't you trying to stop me? What are you laughing about?"

"Oh, it's nothing," he said. "It's just that part of the wall is made of Portentia. And she told me a legend I'd never heard. It's funny!"

Ming snarled loudly. "I *hate* legends. What was it? Portentia, speak!"

All of a sudden, the wall seemed to talk.

"Sorry to darken your bliss,
But the ancient legend goes like this:
'Whoever opens the door to Mokarto,
Will be blasted completely apart-o!'"

Ming stepped back, the key quivering in her claw. Turning to her brother, she said, "Ving, how about you do the honors?"

He didn't move. "Oh, let me think about that. Mmm, no."

"Perhaps Mokarto will *not* open today," said the wizard, still chuckling. "How's that for a *sting*, Ming? Who has tricked who?"

Ming's eye grew steely cold. All at once, she began to smile. "Except that Mokarto's gate *will* open. And you will open it! Or rather, Gelna will open it!"

The wizard gasped. "No! Not her!"

"Gelna?" said Keeah. "Who's that?"

They soon found out. Ming produced a silver amulet from amid her feathers. The moment the wizard saw it, he grew pale.

"You wouldn't dare!" he said.

"Oh, wouldn't I?" She gave it a flick, and a sharp purple beam shot at the wizard.

"Noooo!" Galen yelled.

As the purple smoke enveloped him, the blue-cloaked, white-bearded figure spun and spun. He cried out, and his cry went higher and higher, until when the smoke cleared, he was no longer a figure in blue and white.

He was not even a *he*!

Standing before the Mokarto gate was none other than a white-haired wizard with a pretty face, red lips, and long eyelashes.

"Gelna!" cried Max. "Oh, dear. Not her!"

"Who is she?" asked Neal.

"Gelna is Galen as if he were his own sister," said Max. "And she's a silly sister, too! She does whatever you tell her to! Making Galen into Gelna is how Ming tricked him the first time!"

"One trick after another!" groaned Eric.

The pink-cloaked wizard rearranged her robes and smiled a glittering smile. "Hel*lo*, everyone! It's been *such* a long *time*!"

"Plus, she talks strangely," Max added.

Ming stepped slowly over to her. "Gelna, dear, open the gate to Mokarto, would you? We'll just stand back a little bit."

Gelna clapped her hands together as if it were her birthday. "Oh, *may* I?"

Ming handed her the golden key. "Opening that gate will begin a new Shadow Time for Droon. A time of pirates!"

"And bandits," said Ving.

"A time of raiding ships!" said Ming.

"And castles," added Ving.

"A time for pretty princesses like *me*!"

"And me!" said Ving. "Except for the pretty princess part. Gelna, open that door!"

Gelna approached the door and rapped on it. "*Hawky* hawks, get *ready* to wake *uh-up*!"

Humming, she put the key into the lock. Giggling, she began to turn it.

Ten

The Trickster and the Tricked

"Ho-ho-ho!" Ving laughed. "Such a party we'll have!"

Eric couldn't believe that there was nothing they could do. There were so many hawk creatures, and his friends were so mixed up with them, he couldn't blast them free even if he wanted to. He watched Gelna begin to turn the key in the lock. "Stooopppp!" he yelled.

"My sentiments, exactly!" boomed a

voice from atop the great wheel. "Gelna dear, stop."

Gelna stopped turning the key. "*Okay*!"

Ming squeaked. "What? What? What!"

Everyone looked up. And there, his familiar midnight-colored cloak flying in the wind from the sea, stood Galen himself. His fabulous staff shot sparks of every color from its flaming tip.

Keeah gasped. "But . . . but . . ."

Galen grinned from ear to ear. "Simple, everyone. Ming charmed the wrong man!"

Twisting her bird head one way, then another, Ming stared at Galen, then at Gelna. "So if he's Galen, then who are *you*?"

"Allow *me*, dearie!" chirped Gelna. The pink wizard spun on her high heels for a second and — *whoomf!* — vanished. Nelag stood there instead, wearing his usual blue cloak and hat.

"Sorry, pirate lady," he said with a chuckle. "This time, we tricked *you*."

Without another word, Nelag popped the key under his hat, his favorite pilka flew down the hill, and he was on it — backward — in an instant.

Flink joined him and sang, "Fly, pilka, fly!"

Ming yelled, "This makes me want to —"

"Have a big battle!" shouted Ving.

"Then a battle you shall have!" said Galen.

The hawkmen charged at once.

"We have our own army!" cried Gryndal. "Hee-ya, elves!"

The hog elves leaped into action. They were everywhere at once. Some of them were no taller than bowling pins, but they were brave.

At the same time, a horn sounded, and

the Ninns appeared, rushing up from the shore and into the fray.

"Now that the Ninns are here," boomed the captain, "this battle *really* begins!"

"Pirates, with me," shouted Ming. She opened her wings and took to the air after Nelag and Flink. "Follow that twinkly light!"

"To the soarwings!" yelled Eric.

Neal snatched his turban back from Icthos and raced for the soarwings with his friend.

"Dogfight!" he said. "Against the birds!"

In seconds, the two friends were up in the air after Ming. Eric felt complete again for the first time in hours. His full self was back.

It felt good.

The white birds dived as Ming swooped after Nelag and Flink.

"Faster! Faster!" Eric cried.

Neal zoomed next to him. "I love this!"

Meanwhile, Ving flew up to the mill wheel with a single bound, but Galen was on him in a moment. Laughing, the wizard whipped his staff around and hammered Ving's legs. The magic staff whistled and shimmered with light. Together the two foes fought claw to staff all the way down and right back up to the top of the giant wheel.

Keeah and Julie were their own army. The princess blasted violet sparks here and there, driving the bandits farther back from the golden walls. Julie zoomed over their heads, herding them into a crowd.

Max scurried around at the foot of the giant walls. "Hurry, everyone, the sun is going down. Mokarto will stand forever a silent city of magic stones!"

"There's still time," said Gryndal. "Elves! Put the stones in and turn the wheels the opposite way! Hurry!"

With one great blow of his staff, Galen toppled Ving to the ground. "And the bird falls!"

"This bird is out of here!" said Ving, leaping into the air.

"Oh, no you don't!" cried Julie. She shot after him like a rocket and leaped on his back, forcing him to the ground.

Eric and Neal flew between Nelag and Flink and Ming. They swung the soarwings around and flew straight into the pack of flying pirates.

"Arrrh!" The pirates tumbled to earth, too.

Galen hurled his magic staff once more. It tangled in Ming's wings as she tried to escape. The pirate princess was hurled into a groaning heap with her twin brother.

"Ahh! Get off me!" cried the prince.

"*You* get off *me*!" shouted Ming.

"Why don't you *both* get off?" boomed

Galen. "Right back to where you belong! As long as we're doing tricks, here's a final one!"

He pulled out the little blue bottle he had hidden in his cloak that morning and uncorked it. All at once, the giant wave blew out of the bottle's spout and covered the sky.

"Water? I *hate* water!" cried Ving. "Fly! Ahhhh!"

Whoosh-shoosh-splooosh! The storm scooped up the hawk bandits and their fellow pirates and hurled them, heaved them, threw them up into the purple sky.

"Back to Tarkoom!" yelled Keeah.

"For another four hundred years, I hope!" said Galen, shaking the last drops from the little bottle.

The hawk creatures were swallowed up in the purple cloud like water down a drain. The whole cloud dissolved behind them.

Before twilight had settled over Droon, every last bandit and pirate was gone.

Everything went still and was quiet except for the sound of the huge wheel turning backward. Now when the stones slid onto the earth, they were back to their old selves again. The white tower of Zorfendorf, the Ring of Giants, the age-old cobbled walls of Doobesh, the chunk of Galen's tower, even Portentia herself sat on the dusty plain.

When the sun finally set, every stone was as it was before.

"Gryndal, you did it!" cried Keeah.

"You don't work in Feshu for a full year and not learn something!" the king of the hog elves explained proudly.

"We did it," said Galen. "All of us together. A very successful day, I think. A challenge met in triumph!"

Under Gryndal's direction, the elves

loaded up the soarwings and began the massive job of returning the stones to their original places all over Droon. Over Max's objections, even the frightening white tusks from the Horns of Ko went back to where they belonged.

Because, as Galen said, "Fair is fair."

The Ninns gazed out to the churning black waves of the Serpent Sea.

"We go in search of Sparr again," said the captain, adjusting his armor. Without another word, the red warriors tramped to their ships and took to the icy waters once more.

A few moments later, the stone mills of Feshu went still, and the plains were silent and empty as before.

Galen sighed. "And so, the trickster has become the tricked."

"You tricked us, too!" said Keeah.

"Sorry, friends," he said. "It was essential that you be fooled, too. Ming is so clever, only this could fool her." He turned to Portentia. "Quite the little actress you are, as well."

The stone seemed to beam. "Thank you much, my friendly wizard. Being a wall beats being a lizard!"

Eric finally got his chance to ask the oracle about his vision. "Portentia, who visited me?"

The stone was quiet a moment, then said, "I see not a face, not a nose, not an ear. But the figure moves closer. Soon all will be clear!"

Flink twinkled in to say that she had taken the key safely to Galen's tower, that the tower was back again, whole, in Jaffa City, and that the magical staircase had just appeared behind the mill.

As the friends gathered together at the bottom of the stairs, Flink whispered a final word in Galen's ear, and he began to smile.

"A message from the king and queen," said the wizard. "They've discovered the long-lost forests of Jabar-Loo! Neal, tighten that turban of yours. I smell a new adventure. It won't be long before you join us again!"

"Now those are really good words!" said Neal.

When the three friends said good-bye and started up the stairs, Eric's skin tingled like it had in Mokarto. He stopped and turned.

"Holy cow, you guys. Look!"

In the distant sky, swirling over the farthest reaches of the Droon Sea, was a patch of moving cloud. Only this time it wasn't purple.

It was a bright silvery green.

"Another rift in time?" asked Max.

"That was in the red book, too," said Keeah. "It's called the Green Twilight. It happens when someone comes into Droon . . . from the future!"

"Another guest," said Nelag.

"And another new adventure!" said Julie.

Waving good-bye once more, the three friends raced up the stairs for home.

Just before they stepped into his closet, Eric turned and sniffed the air one last time.

Drifting in the wind and up the stairs was the scent of apples.

Eric smiled to himself. "Soon," he whispered.

Soon he'd know who the dark figure from his vision was.